MP

D0049254

Other Books about Rosy Cole

Watch Out, World—
Rosy Cole is Going Green!

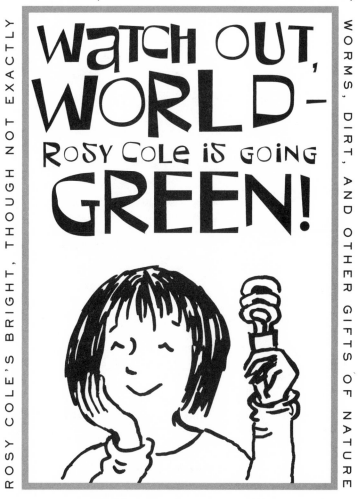

POPULAR, IDEAS ABOUT GARBAGE, WORMS, DIRT, AND OTHER GIFTS OF NATURE

ROSY COLE'S BRIGHT, THOUGH NOT EXACTLY

WATCH OUT, WORLD –
ROSY COLE IS GOING GREEN!

SHEILA GREENWALD

Farrar Straus Giroux
New York

For James George Green

Text and pictures copyright © 2010 by Sheila Greenwald
All rights reserved
Distributed in Canada by D&M Publishers, Inc.
Printed in February 2010 in the United States of America
by RR Donnelley & Sons Company, Bloomsburg, Pennsylvania
Designed by Barbara Grzeslo
First edition, 2010
1   3   5   7   9   10   8   6   4   2

www.fsgkidsbooks.com

Library of Congress Cataloging-in-Publication Data
Greenwald, Sheila.
    Watch out world, Rosy Cole is going green! / Sheila
Greenwald.— 1st ed.
        p.   cm.
    Summary: Rosy's team comes up with some creative ideas for
the Read School Fall Fair, whose mission is to sell "green-
themed" products.
    ISBN: 978-0-374-36280-5
    [1. Green movement—Fiction.   2. Environmental protection—
Fiction.   3. Schools—Fiction.   4. Fairs—Fiction.]   I. Title.

PZ7.G852Wat 2010
[Fic]—dc22

                                                    2008055563

CONTENTS

Watch Out, World—
Rosy Cole is Going Green!

THE BEST IDEA OF MY ENTIRE LIFE

It was finally the day of Miss Read's School Fall Fair. My team had just finished setting up our booth when Mrs. Oliphant, our teacher, told us to take it down.

"Immediately," she said. "Before the headmistress arrives." She looked nervously toward the door of the gym for Headmistress Craft.

"But you gave your approval," I said, trying to stay calm. "We worked so hard to put it together."

"And now please take it apart. I'm sorry. How on earth did all this happen?"

Had she forgotten so soon? It was only a month ago that I dreamt up the *best* idea of my entire life . . .

1

Nature's Gifts

In the middle of the first week of school, Mrs. Oliphant reminded us of the date and theme of Miss Read's School Fall Fair.

"This year the fair hopes to raise enough money to plant trees in the yard and buy energy-saving lightbulbs for the entire school," she said. "Our class has been assigned four different booths to sell green-themed products. Let's come up with some great ideas."

Natalie Pringle raised her hand. "I can bring two dozen copies of the new DVD *Captain Nature*," she called out.

Natalie's father owns Dave's DVDs on Third Avenue.

"Fantastic," Mrs. Oliphant said. "Team one, DVDs and CDs with a nature theme."

"How about books?" Mimi Prescott asked. "I can get forty copies of the best seller *Earth on a High Wire*."

Mimi's mother is Betsy of Betsy's Books on Madison.

"Excellent," Mrs. Oliphant agreed,

adding green-themed books to her list.

"I'm sure many of you will find items to add to Natalie and Mimi's teams." She looked around the room. "Any other team ideas?"

Posey Bloom raised her hand. "Plants, flowers, and shrubs."

Posey's grandparents own Posey's Blooms on Fifth.

Mrs. Oliphant beamed. "How many of you could bring in a cutting from a plant to help out Posey's team?"

Several hands went up.

Mrs. Oliphant smiled at the rest of us. "I bet if you search your rooms, all of you will come up with something you no longer need that could be recycled and would make a great green gift."

Something in my room that I no longer needed that would make a great green gift? I pictured my room.

There wasn't a thing I didn't need.

Except maybe . . .

I remembered the pail full of smelly shells and rocks I had tossed in the back of my closet at the end of summer. Things I had picked up at the beach. My mother called this stuff "nature's gifts."

I raised my hand.

"What about nature's gifts?" I asked.

"What about them?" Mrs. Oliphant looked puzzled.

"Rocks, shells, and sea glass I found on the beach," I explained, thinking how I would need to give them a little touch-up with nail polish to make them look as shiny as they had when they were wet.

"An imaginative idea!" Mrs. Oliphant said. "In fact, we can call your team 'Nature's Gifts.'" Now we have four good teams to choose from. Think about which one you want to join, get together, select a captain, and collect the items you will offer for sale in your booth."

I couldn't believe it. I had come up with a team theme.

"Remember, working as a team means sharing ideas and getting along as a group," Mrs. Oliphant said.

I looked around the room and hoped somebody would sign up to share ideas and get along with me.

At lunch Christy McCurry leaned across the table and put her face next to mine. "Nature's Gifts?" she scoffed. "I think I'll go with Natalie or Mimi's team, or maybe even Posey's."

"That's a good plan," I said, "if you have no *imagination*."

"I have an imagination," Hermione Wong piped up. "I also have rock samples from a nature walk that I don't think anybody would pay a nickel for."

"Rocks?" I remembered the ones I'd seen in the gift shop near my aunt's beach house. "I think you mean doorstops and paperweights painted with happy faces and flowers, then personalized with people's names." I closed my eyes and smiled. "Imagination."

"Maybe I could sell my last batch of fudge," Debby Prusock teased. "It came out hard as a rock."

"Stones that melt in your mouth," Hermione joked.

Even though they laughed, I opened my notebook and wrote this down. Suddenly everyone was so quiet I could practically hear their brains changing gears.

"How about driftwood?" Keisha Wilson called out from the end of the table.

"Woodwork by waves," I said.

Then everyone started talking at the same time, remembering all kinds of rainy day projects from camp that were collecting dust in the back of a closet.

I could hardly write fast enough. "These are all Nature's Gifts," I said, remembering the team name Mrs. Oliphant had suggested.

"You should call my brother, Donald," Christy suggested. "His ammonite collection is huge. How many fossilized sea creatures does one person need anyway? I bet he could spare a few for a good cause."

A good cause? Had Christy changed her mind about my team?

"Ammonites." I wrote this down, happy to have any excuse to call Christy's cool older brother.

"Isn't this amazing?" I asked. "We just started, and already we're sharing ideas and working like a team. And we'll have loads of stuff to sell, too."

"Not loads," Linda Dildine shook her head. "All I have is tree fungus," she confessed.

"Don't worry," I assured her. "If you open your eyes to nature, you'll find gift ideas all around you."

"Open your eyes at the American Museum of Natural History gift shop and you'll find even more," Hermione advised. "They've got the best gifts from nature you ever saw."

Since Hermione is a regular at the museum and its gift shop, I would take her word for it.

"The fair is October 20," I said, closing my notebook. "That's only a little over a month away. If you're interested in the Nature's Gifts team, our first meeting will be next Thursday at my place."

"Aye, aye, captain," Debby said, saluting me.

I sat there, smiling. Who would believe an idea that started with a pail of smelly beach stuff would take off like a seagull following a garbage barge? I could just imagine myself at the helm in the captain's chair!

My name is Rosy Cole. I live on the Upper East Side of Manhattan in the same building as Hermione Wong and Christy McCurry. We attend Miss Read's School, which is all girls and private. My two older sisters, who went to Read, tell me that as far back as they can remember, the Fall Fair with its raffles and games and booths was always the same. People like Natalie and Jenny and Posey bring expensive new things everybody wants, and people like me bring outgrown T-shirts and old toys that end up on the junk heap.

But I had a feeling that with a little luck, this year would be completely different.

2

GOING GREEN

As soon as I got home from school, I sprayed Love Me Tonight on my wrists and called Donald McCurry.

"Would you have any ammonites to donate to our Nature's Gifts team for the fair?" I asked.

"I guess I could spare a few of the smaller ones," he offered. "But they aren't very colorful."

"That's okay," I assured him. "It doesn't matter if they're colorful or not. I plan to paint them with special little messages."

"Paint them!" Donald groaned. "You mean something like 'Hi there, I'm an ammonite. Aren't I cute?'"

"It so happens that when you inscribe rocks with words like 'Imagination' and 'Peace' and 'Serenity,' they're much more appealing," I informed him.

"Listen, Rosy, rocks and fossils are appealing without paint or words on them," Donald argued. "In fact, they are among the most amazing things on the planet. I could show you some boulders in Central Park that contain mica and quartz and garnet. They were pushed here all the way from Canada by a giant glacier thousands of years ago.

"I'm sure they're very nice," I said, trying to be polite. "But Central Park boulders are a little big for my booth. Your ammonites would be just right."

"I'll think about it," Donald said, suddenly sounding colder than any giant Canadian glacier.

Sometimes I don't know why I like Donald. Even though he makes my insides fizzy as soda water, he sometimes makes me feel silly and stupid. Still, Donald thinking about helping me was better than Donald *not* thinking about helping me.

I was sure he would. I was sure he would come around once he saw how good our booth looked. I had a feeling that with a little imagination, nature that's just lying around for free could be made into something even better— something good enough to sell at a school fair that's raising money to go green.

That night at dinner, I told my family about our team.

"Well done!" my sister Pippa congratulated me. "I'm glad to hear that someone in this family will care about the environment while we're away at college. We all need to go green."

My mother sighed. "I don't have time to go green right now. I'm too busy."

"Are you too busy to carry a shopping bag that isn't plastic?" Pippa asked. "Are you too busy to hang-dry clothes washed in cold water with green detergent?"

"Stop lecturing your mother," Dad scolded. "After managing a law office four days a week, she comes home to shop and cook. She took extra pains over this dinner so you two would have a great send-off."

Pippa glared at the shrimp on the

end of her fork. "This was flown here from halfway around the world on a plane that spewed deadly fumes into the air we breathe."

My mother stopped eating.

"Please, Mom. Make an effort to buy local," Anitra said, taking Mom's hand.

"You mean pick tomatoes from that patch in the lobby and catch fish out of the courtyard fountain?" Dad tried to joke.

But no one laughed.

· · ·

As soon as we finished dinner, Anitra and Pippa began clearing out their closets and drawers, packing for college. It seemed that what they weren't taking with them, they were throwing away.

"How can I wear these leather boots anymore?" Pippa exclaimed, tossing them in the garbage. "They were once a sweet cow."

"And my old makeup and nail polish." Anitra dumped all the little bottles into the trash. "Toxic."

"Those hobby kits contain poisonous dyes," Pippa warned when she saw me take them out of the trash bag. "Don't be fooled by the pictures on the box."

I wasn't fooled. I was excited. The hobby kits and nail polish would be perfect for turning seashells and sea glass into beautiful pendants.

When Pippa finished sorting through her things, she presented Mom with a canvas shopping bag.

Anitra tacked a list of rules to the kitchen bulletin board.

"This should be a real help to you, Mom," Pippa said, looking pleased with herself. "And, Rosy, you could share this list with your green team."

I didn't tell her I already had my own list.

3

How to Catch a Local Critter

Saturday morning when I asked permission to go to the museum, my mother was delighted.

"I'm so pleased this project has inspired you to explore the world of natural history," she said, opening her purse to find money for my ticket.

I didn't explain that what I wanted to explore wasn't the world of natural history, but how to sell natural history to the world!

The minute we walked into the gift shop, I could see that Hermione was right. All the ideas we needed were right here.

There were some gifts we had thought of and some we hadn't.

"Over here is my favorite spot in the entire museum," Hermione confided, pulling me up the stairs to the bookshop.

"Books?" I asked.

"And the people who read them," she said with a sly smile. Then I remembered that Hermione has always dreamed of having a brainy boyfriend.

By the time we were ready to leave, I was happy we had come. And when I saw Donald waiting in the ticket line, I thought I was in natural history heaven.

"This is Pete," Donald said, introducing us to the boy next to him. "He's a science nut like me."

Hermione grabbed my arm. *"And me,"* she cooed.

"Are you here to see the live butter-flies?" Pete asked her.

"No, alas." Hermione groaned as if she had lost a loved one. "Though the living butterfly exhibit is the most thrilling thing I've ever seen, my friend here insisted we check out the store instead."

"The *store*?" Pete looked confused.

"Rosy only likes nature if it's gift-wrapped," Donald explained. "Ammonites aren't good enough for her unless they have cute messages written on them. Rosy likes nature when it's dead—and has a price tag."

"That's not true," I objected. "I wouldn't mind if your ammonites were alive."

"*Live* ammonites!" Pete gasped.

"Why not?" I asked.

"Maybe because they became extinct with the dinosaurs, over sixty-five million years ago," Donald said.

For a minute I wished I'd gone extinct with the dinosaurs, too.

"Fooled you." I tried to laugh, hoping nobody would guess who was the fool.

Then I tried changing the subject. "Even if ammonites aren't alive, it would be great if our booth could sell live creature habitats like the ant farms in the museum shop."

"I have a book you could borrow that tells how to catch a local critter," Pete told me. "I'll drop it off with Donald."

"A beautiful, fascinating, exotic local creature is something I have always wanted to catch," Hermione said, gazing at Pete as if he had just sprouted antennae and six legs. "Since I live in Donald's building, you can drop off your book with me, Hermione Wong."

"Hey, we're next in line," Donald said, pulling Pete away.

As they hurried off, I took hold of Hermione to keep her from running after them with an imaginary butterfly net.

4

Two Thousand Little Wigglers

Sunday morning when the phone rang and Mom told me it was Donald Mc-Curry, I guessed he had decided to offer me some ammonites for our Nature's Gifts booth after all.

"If you're serious about selling live critter habitats, you don't need Pete's book," Donald said. "I can help. Why don't you stop by?"

Was Donald competing with his friend to be helpful? Was he actually jealous? I didn't bother with the elevator. I flew down the stairs.

Donald was waiting for me at his door. "Take a look at this," he said, handing me a booklet as I followed him to his room.

"These worms are nature's wonder workers. They compost city garbage and make it into rich topsoil," Donald explained.

"What could be better?" I said, trying not to look at the picture of the worms.

Donald beamed his approval. "Since you understand how great they are, I wonder if you would help me out."

"Why not?" I said. "That's what friends are for."

I actually thought Donald might give me a hug.

"I need a little time to educate my folks," he said. "It would be a real help if you would prepare their bedding while I prepare Mom and Dad for them."

"Them?" I sat down.

"The two thousand red wigglers I sent away for," he nodded. "That's how many you need to compost the garbage of a family of four."

"Two thousand worms?"

"Since the directions say wood is best, you need something like an old trunk or barrel or even a dresser drawer lined with damp shredded newspaper. Then all you have to do is fill it with eggshells, vegetable peels, and coffee grounds, and add a little dirt on top."

"You want me to make beds out of garbage for two thousand worms?" I was beginning to feel a little sick.

"It would just be so the worms have a home when they arrive. I need a little time to convince my parents of how fantastic they are—putting organic matter back into the soil and reducing the number of landfills that are taking over the planet."

"I don't understand how this helps our booth," I mumbled, standing up and heading for the door before I got sicker.

"If all goes well, I could spare you a few hundred to sell for starter kits," Donald called after me. "They multiply like crazy."

Out in the hall, waiting for the elevator to take me back upstairs, I tried not to think of two thousand worms multiplying like crazy.

5

My idea Grows Wings

At our first Nature's Gifts team meeting, everyone placed their products on my bed except for Hermione.

"Mine is a surprise," she explained, clutching a paper bag to her chest.

"I love what you did to your tree fungus," I said, complimenting Linda on the "Fun Gus" faces she'd drawn.

"And the driftwood dancers with their painted ballet shoes are adorable," Debby told Keisha.

When we were finished admiring one another's work, it was finally Hermione's turn.

"Ta da," she sang as she slowly lifted a box from the paper bag. "Guess what?"

"Pasta?" Debby guessed.

"Look again," Hermione laughed. "And you will see it's not just noodles."

"Mealworms?" Debby wrinkled her nose. "Those revolting little things that get into cereal?"

"Ants are revolting little things that get into sugar bowls," Hermione pointed out. "But put them in a see-through container and call it an ant farm and someone will spring $15.95 for the pleasure of taking them home."

"Fifteen dollars and ninety-five cents?" Christy gasped.

"But it's not just about money," Hermione insisted. "Pete says we couldn't live on this planet without bugs. My mealworms are the amazing larval stage of an insect that will soon morph and evolve into mealworm beetles." She showed us the book Pete had lent her. "This book has changed my life."

Hermione read from the first page. "All you need for this great insect adventure is a magnifying glass, nets,

jars with holes in the lids, and tweezers."

My team was so quiet you could
practically hear the mealworms chew.

"Keep reading," Linda demanded.

"You can find what you're looking for
in the air, around water, soil, or plants,
and near animals or food." She held up
the book to show us the pictures.

"It's like going on a safari," Debby
said.

"Exactly," Hermione agreed. "Signs
of life are everywhere. Just look
around you."

"Something has been eating holes in my sweaters," Debby recalled.

"Maybe it's a wool moth," Hermione said.

"We have a desk my Dad wants to fumigate," Linda suddenly remembered.

"Powder post beetles, if you're lucky," Hermione told her.

Christy was sure she had spotted fruit flies swarming around some peaches.

"I can't wait to see what I find," Keisha said, pulling on her jacket. "This could be more fun than a treasure hunt."

"*A treasure hunt?* For things we spray and swat and step on?" I began to laugh.

But nobody laughed with me. They were too busy packing up their gifts from nature so they could race home and start hunting.

"Phone me if you need advice," Hermione called out to the team. She handed me Pete's book. "I don't need this anymore," she said as she went out the door. "Just follow the directions and you'll be sure to find a tiny creature about to morph and change into something totally new."

I hoped she was right. If not, I had a feeling that the only creature I would observe morphing and changing would be Hermione Wong becoming the new captain of my team.

I had no time to lose.

6

A Real Friend

Fortunately, it looked like all I had to do was follow the directions in Pete's book about city bugs and I would be sure of success.

What You Need
1. Magnifying glass
2. Nets
3. Jars with holes in the lids
4. Tweezers

Where to Look
1. In the air
2. Around water
3. Around soil, plants, animals, and food

On Monday, after I searched the air all afternoon, Debby called to report she had caught her wool moth.

On Tuesday, I tried looking in water and Linda bagged a powder post beetle.

On Wednesday, it was soil, plants, animals, and food.

Then Keisha came up with another mealworm habitat and Christy landed a fruit fly.

Thursday morning, I finally caught a bug of my own.

Unfortunately, it kept me home from school for a few days. I took medicine and dreamt about its habitat.

Friday afternoon, Donald called. "I have to see you right now," he whispered before I could say a word. "Something has come up."

"Yes, it has," I agreed. "I've changed my mind about the red wigglers. I'd even like a few to sell in our booth."

Two minutes later, he was on the landing carrying a large plastic bin.

"I knew you'd come through," Donald said. "Do you have a good place for them?" He glanced at the piano. "Wood is best."

I led him past my door to my sisters' room.

"Are you sure they'll be safe?" Donald asked.

"Anitra and Pippa took everything with them to college. They won't be home till Thanksgiving," I assured him.

"This is great," Donald said when I showed him not one perfect spot but two. "My mother doesn't appreciate these worms. Until she changes her mind, they should be happy here." He

lined Anitra's and Pippa's underwear drawers with strips of wet newspaper. Finally, he turned his bin over. Out into the drawers came orange peels, eggshells, apple cores, and dirt.

But that wasn't all.

"What if my mother doesn't appreciate worms, either?" I asked, half hoping she wouldn't.

"Don't worry, they'll only need to stay till my parents see the light," Donald promised. "Meanwhile, it's up to you to keep them moist and fed and aired." He put out his hand to shake. "It's up to both of us to keep them our secret."

Before he left, Donald gave me six small ammonites. "I'll never forget this favor, Rosy," he told me. "You've been a real friend."

So now, all because two thousand red wiggler worms were chomping away on garbage in my sisters' underwear drawers, I was Donald's real friend. And we even shared a secret.

It was enough to completely change my mind about those little red wigglers.

7

Eco Babe!

That night after dinner, I told my parents I would take care of our garbage. They both thanked me. "I always mean to recycle," Mom said. "I just don't have time."

Dad found an extra pail for glass, plastic, and metal, while I gathered papers into a neat heap. "You are setting an example for both of us," he said.

Out on our back landing, I separated vegetable and fruit scraps from meat and dairy. After all, worms are vegan. In our neighbors' trash there was everything I'd need for worm starter kits.

Before I went to bed, I took care of my worms. Watching them chow down reminded me of characters in a fairy tale. Only instead of spinning straw into gold overnight, they would begin to turn garbage into rich topsoil in only three months' time. Fortunately, because my sisters were gone, they could do this in private.

Saturday morning, I called everyone on my team. "I have some amazing live critters," I announced. "But I can't tell you what they are yet."

Christy was suspicious. "I hope you didn't buy a kit for hatching butterflies. They're not local, so that wouldn't be fair."

"I didn't buy anything," I told her. "Who would do such a thing?"

"Donald," Christy said, lowering her voice. "He sent off for some worms. Mom and Dad were furious. They said they didn't care if our garbage turned into rich topsoil in just three months. They don't need rich topsoil. So they ordered Donald to get rid of the wigglers, immediately."

"I wonder what he did with them," I said, happy Christy couldn't see me grinning into the phone.

"We think he gave the worms to Pete," Christy went on. "Donald loved them so much; he'd only trust his best friend."

His best friend?

Later, I called Donald to let him know his worms and his secret were safe with me.

"I think my parents are beginning to come around," Donald said. "But I'll never forget this favor."

"That's what best friends are for," I told him.

Monday morning, Mrs. Oliphant asked how our team was shaping up.

"We're adding live habitats to the rocks, leaves, shells, and glass and wood products we'll be selling," I said.

"You mean like ant farms?" Mrs. Oliphant asked.

I nodded, without mentioning that unlike the ant farms at the museum store, our habitats would come with real critters!

At lunch, Bunny Price, senior editor of *The Read-O-Reader*, sat down at our table. "Your teacher says your team is working together so well, doing original and creative work," she said. "Tell me about it so I can write a story for the school paper."

Everyone crowded around.

"Along with gifts created from nature—like amazing rock doorstops and jewelry made of shells and sea glass—

we will sell nature itself," Hermione said.

"Like my fruit fly farm," Christy explained. "One of nature's miracles."

"Not compared to powder posts," Linda argued. "Their eggs hatch into tiny larvae which bore holes into wood. They can live for over four years."

"Fruit flies can live on anything," Christy boasted. "One pair can produce enough offspring to fill the space between the earth and the sun."

"I've read critters that produce like that have small brains and don't live

long," Debby snapped. "Only two months," she added, eyeing Christy with suspicion. "My wool moths lay only forty or fifty eggs that hatch in four days. They are so gifted they are able to spin wonderful silky little mats from bits of cloth. When it comes to interesting behavior, wool moths are tops."

"Won't you miss your insects after they're sold?" Bunny wanted to know.

"We've taken photos of them to put in an album," Debby said. "We're calling it Earth's Teensy Friends."

"But you're right. Pictures won't help when they're gone." Linda shook her head. Then she sighed. "The truth is, I don't want to sell them."

"Me neither," Christy agreed, her eyes filling with tears. "Even if they live only two months, I have their little babies to look forward to."

"You two are way too emotional," Hermione scolded. "Pete says people who study insects are called entomologists. What they do is science, not a soap opera. Scientists don't get all weepy about their work."

"You have no heart!" Christy fired back. Without any warning, she picked up her tray and stormed off to another table. After a moment, Linda joined her.

Then, all together, Hermione, Debby, and Keisha pulled back their chairs and marched out of the lunchroom.

My teammates were gone, but Bunny was still taking notes.

"Team conflicts," I heard her mutter. "A struggle for power." She closed her notebook. "I'd love to observe your next meeting. Team dynamics are *so* interesting."

I told her she would be welcome, though after what just happened I worried how our next meeting would go and what her headlines might say.

As it turned out, I didn't need to worry about the meeting. Bunny was the only one to show up. Since nobody else was around, she interviewed Mom.

"Rosy has influenced us to go green," Mom boasted, showing off our garbage pails. "Even though it was her sisters who left me a list of rules to follow, it was Rosy who started us off recycling. I only wish there was some way to compost."

I thought of how happy she would be when I showed her there was.

"You've done a great job educating your mom," Bunny said. "You're a real eco babe."

An eco babe! How cool!

That night I was so excited I couldn't fall asleep, so I tiptoed into my sisters' room to check on my wigglers. Carefully, I opened the drawers. There they were, gorging away in the dark, a band of tiny miracle workers.

I got back into bed and closed my eyes.

Maybe *The Read-O-Reader* was just the beginning.

I was certain that when the Nature's Gift team found out we were about to be famous, it would bring us together again.

But when I saw Hermione and Christy waiting for me in the lobby the next morning, I knew we didn't need fame to unite us. We had tragedy.

"I put my critters in the fridge so they would go dormant," Hermione sniffled, "and instead they died. They never got to the pupal stage."

"I read that they'd only live two months, but I didn't believe it," Christy blubbered. "There were no babies."

When we got to school, it turned out the powder posts and wool moths had gone the way of the mealworms and fruit flies.

"Was it a suicide pact?" Keisha wondered.

"You were right," Linda said to Hermione and Debby. "We weren't scientific. We treated them like virtual pets on a Web site."

"At least virtual pets don't die on you and break your heart," Christy moaned.

"What good are they now?" Hermione asked.

I thought for a moment. "Earth's Teensy Friends postcards?" I suggested tactfully.

"Postcards?" Linda yelped. "Turn our little mites into postcards?"

Everyone stopped crying.

"Like the exhibit at the Museum of Natural History," I quickly explained.

"Only instead of sticking dead bugs to the wall, we'll tape them onto file cards and add their scientific names and facts and then Xerox the cards and sell them as a complete set. It would be a way to honor them."

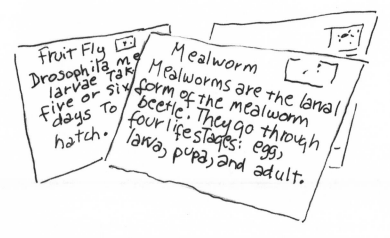

Fruit Fly
Drosophila me
larvae Tak
five or six
days To
hatch.

Mealworm
Mealworms are the larval form of the mealworm beetle. They go through four life stages: egg, larva, pupa, and adult.

"Postcards and albums are okay," Linda said, sniffling again, "but unless Rosy really has an amazing mystery critter to show us at the fair, all the buzz has gone out of our Nature's Gifts booth."

"When the time is right and I no longer need to keep them secret, I will introduce you to my critters. You won't be disappointed," I promised.

Later, I called Donald to report on the wigglers. "They're the best," I said. "Healthy and happy and they do great work—unlike some other bugs I could name."

"My folks are beginning to come around," he said. "I don't think it will be long before I have them convinced."

This was good news and bad news. I'd be able to reveal the secret at last. But I would miss feeding and watching over my new little friends.

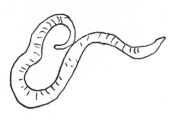

8

Surprise!

Since our very last meeting of Nature's Gifts was also Keisha's birthday, I asked my mother to pick up a surprise birthday cake.

Another surprise was the sound of my sisters' voices as I opened the door.

"We wanted to surprise you and show up at the fair tomorrow," Anitra said, taking off her coat.

"I even skipped a class," Pippa whispered, picking up her duffel bag and heading off to unpack.

Anitra was right behind her.

"Aren't you pleased your sisters made the trip just for you?" Mom asked, leading us into the kitchen.

Pleased?

My hands began to shake and my stomach felt like it was on a wild roller-coaster ride. I could hardly move.

How long would it take till my sisters opened their drawers? If there was anything I could do to stop them, I couldn't think of it.

Mom poured out glasses of juice and lit candles on a pink-and-yellow cake with "Keisha" written on it in chocolate. After everybody sang "Happy Birthday," Keisha closed her eyes. "Quiet," she ordered. "I'm making a wish."

I could hear the clock ticking and my sisters singing as they unzipped their duffel bags. I made a wish of my own, and it had nothing to do with birthdays. Suddenly, my sisters' singing turned to shrieks. In seconds they burst into the kitchen.

"What do you call this?" Pippa screamed.

"Red wiggler worms," I told her, trying to stay calm.

Anitra dropped her underwear drawer so fast that I was afraid my poor worms would die of fright. Then Pippa ran toward the trash pail, making gagging noises.

"Please don't throw them in the garbage," I pleaded.

"They *are* garbage," Anitra said.

"No," I said quickly, "they recycle garbage into topsoil." I turned to Mom. "Donald asked me to keep them just till his folks give him a thumbs-up."

"I thought your booth was shells, rocks, and glass," Mom said with a sigh. "Not worms."

"What's wrong with my brother's worms?" Christy wanted to know. "They're brilliant composters. I'm proud to say that just this morning *my* parents have agreed to try them out."

"Fine," Anitra shouted, handing a

huge plastic bag to Pippa, who held it open so she could dump the worms from her drawer into it. "They can start trying—right now."

"I don't understand," I said. "I thought you cared about going green and working together to save the planet." I turned to Mom. "You said you wished you could compost. That's what red wigglers do."

"Not in my underwear drawer, they don't!" Pippa hissed, handing the plastic bag full of worms to Christy.

"Let me keep just a few and put them in mini beds to sell at the fair," I begged.

Mom shook her head. "Get rid of all those worms," she said. "And promise me right now that you will never bring another critter into this apartment without letting me know first."

I promised.

What difference did it make? I'd lost my little wigglers and all my dreams of having the best booth ever at the Fall Fair.

My team got up from the table. No one had touched the cake. "I have to go home and pack up for the fair," Hermione mumbled as everyone hurried out the door.

At least we still had all our original products to sell. So what if not one of them was a living, breathing creature?

After they were gone, I put the mini-bed starter kits in a box and changed the sign.

From my closet I took the shells, sea glass, ammonites, and rock products I had decorated and turned into jewelry and paperweights and doorstops. Linda was right. They had no buzz. But it was all I had. I pulled out a large empty shopping bag big enough to hold them.

But it turned out the shopping bag was not empty.

I could hardly believe my eyes.

There they were, alive and healthy as could be. Best of all, since I hadn't brought them into the household, I didn't even have to ask Mom's permission. They had been living inside a shopping bag in my very own closet habitat.

I trapped enough for six jars, and called Donald to tell him my news.

"*Blattella germanica?*" he cried. "One of the oldest living creatures on the planet. They have survived earthquakes and volcanoes. You'll even find one on the wall of the Spectrum of Life at the Museum of Natural History."

This I had to see for myself.

. . .

Looking out the window of the crosstown bus as it rode through Central Park, I saw the boulders Donald had talked about. They were huge, with spots of mica that shone in the sunlight. I could see where they had been deeply gouged by other rocks and sediment as they traveled in the ice sheet. Had they really been right here for thousands of years?

I got off the bus and, before heading to the museum, went into the park to see if I could pick up a few small stones. Where had they come from? I wondered if they had started out underwater, and then, like the boulders, had been shoved by a glacier all the way from Canada.

Donald was right. Their history was amazing. They were beautiful, too, even without messages written in nail polish.

When I finally got to the American Museum of Natural History and walked into the Hall of Biodiversity, it was just like Donald had said. There, up on the wall with the myriapods and its fellow insects, was my very own *Blattella germanica*. I was filled with pride to see the relative of my critters under lights, on display in the gallery of a great museum, celebrated as a real player in the history of life on our planet.

As soon as I got home, I checked *Blattella germanica* out in Pete's book. Though they may not be good at composting garbage, they're team players, working together, sharing space, and helping one another. I could hardly wait till the big moment at the fair when I would introduce *them* to my team.

9

A Better Idea

The great day had finally arrived.

But suddenly there was nothing great about it.

At first Mrs. Oliphant said what a fine job we had done. "These DVDs and books should be a sellout. The plants and flowers are beautiful," she had gushed, putting on her glasses for a closer look. "And where are those living critter habitats you told me about, Rosy?"

Linda's eyes filled with tears. "Dead and gone." She'd begun to weep.

"Not all of them," I announced. This

was the moment I had been waiting for. Slowly, I opened my paper bag.

Everyone crowded around to see what was inside.

Mrs. Oliphant peered into a jar as I lifted it from the bag. "What do you call these, anyway?" she asked.

I held the jar up to the light. "*Blattella germanica.*"

"*Blattella germanica?*" Mrs. Oliphant stepped closer. Then she jumped back. "They look like ordinary cockroaches to me!"

"Roaches?" Natalie Pringle began to scream. "Get rid of them before they crawl all over our DVDs and books!"

"Or my plants," Posey shrieked. "How could you bring such *disgusting* things?"

"Disgusting? Blattella germanica? They have a fossil history going back more than three hundred million years," I informed her. "They work together as a team, sharing space and food and water. They're democratic. They have no queen like bees or armies like ants. They even love books!"

"They sure do. Roaches nested in my mom's complete set of Shakespeare and destroyed it," Mimi hissed. "If they settle in here, you can say goodbye to the library."

Mrs. Oliphant put up a hand for silence. "Close down this booth immediately. Before the headmistress arrives."

"But you gave your approval. We worked so hard to put it together," I stammered.

"And now please take it apart. I'm sorry. How on earth did all this happen?"

How could she ask?

"Roaches are repulsive little pests that are good at contaminating everything around them," Mrs. Oliphant went on. "I need you to put all of Nature's Gifts in the courtyard garbage bin."

"That's not fair," Hermione sputtered. "We didn't know Rosy was bringing cockroaches. She did it at the last minute."

"Because I found them at the last minute," I said. "It was my best idea ever."

"Then you better come up with a

better idea *right now*," Christy advised.

"A better idea?"

I looked at the rocks and shells I once thought were so boring that they had to be painted with nail polish, and the bugs I once thought were just something to step on, and I turned over our sign and made a new one—because a better idea is exactly what I had.

"A museum?" Mrs. Oliphant asked. "Why?"

"Because the museum is where I found out going green is about respecting and protecting the earth and *all* its creatures," I explained. "Even the ones that aren't as pretty as butterflies or as cute as ladybugs can teach us important lessons."

"Lessons? What lessons?" Mrs. Oliphant demanded.

"How to survive floods and earthquakes and volcanoes and the poisons we develop to kill them," I said. "How to go without food for up to a month. How to live without doing harm to other insects." I set my *Blattella* habitats at the front of the table. "How to become one of the oldest living creatures on the planet."

Mrs. Oliphant burst out laughing. "Rosy Cole, if there were a prize for most original and creative, this team would surely win it." She looked at the clock on the gym wall. "I see it's ten o'clock. Go ahead. Keep those lids closed tight, but open your museum to the public."

There was no time for my team to celebrate, since friends and family were filling up the gym. A small line formed to check out our museum and its store.

Donald and Pete were right up front. "I thought you could use some of these," Donald said, scooping wigglers out of a bucket and dropping a few in each of my starter beds. "There aren't enough to compost," he apologized.

"But fortunately they multiply like crazy," I said, laughing.

Anitra purchased a box of Debby's Stone Fudge. Pippa decided on a sea glass pendant painted with her old nail polish. Mom and Dad were impressed that I knew anything about rocks.

Posey's grandmother said she'd be interested in Donald's topsoil for her flower shop.

When Headmistress Craft arrived, she took pictures of our booth for the annual school bulletin. "I was once a science teacher," she said. "This would have made such a good class project. I'm sorry I never thought of it. Well done!"

Bunny Price was there, too, with her reporter's notebook. "Congratulations!" she said, her pencil poised. "So what are your plans now, Rosy Cole?"

"There's always next year's fair," I

told her. "Global warming, melting glaciers, and rising sea levels aren't going away anytime soon. Who knows, maybe trees and energy-saving lightbulbs are just the beginning!"

Miss Read's School Goes Greener

Working Together to Compost The Lunchroom

How to Make Your Own
Worm Farm

Want to compost with worms just like Rosy and Donald? It's easy! In just a few simple steps you can turn your garbage into rich fertilizer for your garden—with the help of some wiggly worms, of course!

Step One: Find a Container

There are all different kinds of containers that worms can live in—wooden ones, metal ones, plastic ones—and all different sizes, too. Luckily, worms are not very picky when it comes to where they live. What they like most of all is to be somewhere that is cool, moist, and dark. Rosy and Donald suggest using a plastic tub, about 10 inches deep, 10 inches wide, and 15 inches long. Scrub the tub clean with detergent and warm water before you begin making your worm home, and have an adult drill a few tiny holes in the top and bottom for air circulation and drainage. Don't worry, the worms won't try to escape!

Step Two: Find a Cozy Spot for
Your Worm Home

Rosy chose to put her worms inside Anitra and Pippa's dresser, but now that she thinks about it, that was probably not the best spot. A better choice would be a basement or garage, or outside in a shady location. Wherever you put your worms, make sure it doesn't get too cold or too hot. Worms are happiest at temperatures between 50 and 80 degrees Fahrenheit. If you put the worms outside, be sure to attach a sturdy lid to the container. Worms don't like bugs (or nosy dogs!).

Step Three: Make the Bedding

A worm's favorite type of bedding is shredded-up newspaper. They don't enjoy the colored pages like the comics, though (worms are funny when it comes to the funnies). Black-and-white pages like the classifieds work best. You can also use computer paper shredded into nice thin strips. Fill the bin with the bedding, and add a few handfuls of garden soil. Spray it all with water, until everything is nice and moist, but not so wet that it looks like a lake (worms are not good swimmers). If your worm home gets too wet, just add more newspaper.

Step Four: Add the Worms

This is the most important part, because your garbage won't compost itself! The best kind of worms for composting are redworms, also known as red wigglers or manure worms. Don't use regular nightcrawlers, or garden worms, since they are fussy and don't like living in boxes very much. You can buy redworms from bait shops, garden centers, or online. When you buy the worms, the seller will be able to tell you how many you need for your size container and for the amount of food scraps you want to compost. In general, one pound of food scraps per day is enough to feed two thousand worms!

Step Five: Keep Your Worms Alive
and Happy

Worms will eat just about anything you do, except meat, fish, or dairy products. They especially love coffee grounds and food that's gone bad in the fridge! For a special treat you can give them soaked pieces of ripped-up pizza boxes or crushed eggshells. Yum, yum! Never feed your worms things like metal or Styrofoam. Be sure to keep the worms and their bedding moist (but not wet). After just a few months, your worms will begin to turn the soil and food into rich, healthy castings (which is another word for worm poop, but "castings" sounds much nicer). Use the castings as fertilizer for your garden, and add more bedding and food so your worms can get back to work!

Acknowledgments

Twenty-six years ago Melanie Kroupa encouraged me to write the first of what would become twelve books about Rosy Cole. Her gifts as an editor made my work on these books a journey of discovery and delight for which I am so very grateful.